Bootsie

Just One More

MIKE JAMES

Text copyright © Mike James 2012
ISBN: 978-1-922022-29-5
Published by Vivid Publishing
P.O. Box 948, Fremantle
Western Australia 6959
www.vividpublishing.com.au

Chapters

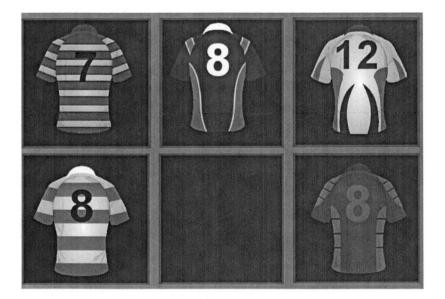

Framed

Bootsie caught the bus home from All Kings for the first time. He was saving his parents from driving all the way down to the school, just to turn around and go back again. Bootsie's mum was already waiting for him when the bus pulled into the main bus station. Bootsie couldn't wait to get off the bus, which he had been on for the last four and a half hours. His mum was very pleased to see him and even tried to carry his suitcase for him until she realised it was way too heavy for her and she left it to her much stronger son.

"Gosh you've grown since the last time I saw you," she said to him as she gave him a hug and a kiss. "How are you?"

"Oh I'm just great. The first time you get me to catch a bus home it breaks down halfway here. I had to sit on the side of the road for an hour waiting for another one. How are you?" Bootsie replied sarcastically.

"Oh you poor thing, that must have been so awful being put out for a whole hour," she replied, with an even more sarcastic voice than her son's. "Let's get you home," she added, as Bootsie got into the passenger seat.

I need a cup of tea. I've been running around all day and haven't had one for ages," she replied with a smile.

"Well come on, what's been happening? I haven't had a letter or a phone call for ages," she said to him as they drove out of the station.

"Oh, not much," he replied.

"Come on, you can do better than that," his mum said to him.

As they travelled the short trip back to the house Bootsie told his mum about different things that had happened in the last few months. He told her about the team's good run into the second half of the season, he also told her about the Pacific Islander schoolboys team that came to the school and how he had another jumper for his collection.

"What's been going on at home?" he asked his mum.

"Umm, let me see, well I've started working again. I've got a job at the hospital doing some nursing again, which is keeping me busy, and you know your dad's job is keeping him away a lot, he's overseas again now. Your sister is doing very well in her netball; I think she's got your sporty genes as well. Other than that, things have been pretty normal," she replied, just as they pulled into the driveway of their house.

Bootsie carried his suitcase and bags inside and dropped them in the lounge room and then proceeded to lie down on the couch.

"Aaah, seven weeks holiday," he said, as he stretched out completely and turned on the TV.

"Is that where you're going to spend it, is it?" asked his mum.

"Yep," he replied.

"Well can you put your suitcase and bags in your room and unpack first?" she asked.

"Yeah, later," he replied.

"No, now!" his mum snapped back.

"Come on Mum, I just got home," Bootsie grumbled.

"Yeah I can see. You've been here a minute and already you've made a mess," his mum added.

"A mess? Where?" he replied.

"Your stuff," she said, as she looked down at the pile of bags and the suitcase. "Come on, put it away now," she said to Bootsie.

"Oh alright," he replied, as he pulled himself off the couch.

Bootsie picked up his bags and his mum followed him down the hall towards his bedroom. He opened the door to his room and couldn't believe his eyes. Firstly, his dad was sitting on his bed, which was great because Bootsie had been sneakily told he was away on business and the second thing was what was on his wall.

"They're fantastic!" he said to his parents as he stared at the main wall in his room. "When did you do this?" he asked them both.

"We picked them up this morning," said his mum.

"And *I* put them up this afternoon," replied his dad. "Do you like them?"

"They're brilliant," replied Bootsie, as he looked at the framed jumpers.

While he'd been away, Bootsie's parents had five of his special jumpers framed behind glass and hung in his bedroom. Against the blue painted wall they really did look fantastic. One jumper was from All Kings with a black number 7 on the back that he had swapped with Razzi when he was at Charlton Hall. In the middle on the top was a Charlton Hall jumper he had swapped in his first year at All Kings. Next to that was the jumper he swapped with the Pacific Islanders' inside centre after the regional game he had played in. On the bottom left was the Southern Region jumper he had swapped after they won the final of the competition. On the bottom right was his first regional jumper that he had worn against the Western Region and for some reason the frame in the middle on the bottom was empty.

"I can put the Pacific Islanders number 8 jumper I got at All Kings in that one," he said to his parents as he looked at the empty frame hanging on the wall.

"Well actually, we hoped that one would be for your first national jumper," his dad replied.

"What a great idea. Hopefully it won't stay empty for too long," Bootsie replied with a smile. "I don't know how I can thank you for doing this," he said to them both.

"Oh Bootsie, you went through so much this year it's our way of saying how proud of you we are, that's all," replied his mum with a huge smile.

"Yeah, hopefully next year will be a lot easier," he replied. The three of them just looked at each other and laughed.

2

The Daily T

Weekend Edition

Rugby's Challenge Cup is or

The regional rugby board last night announced that the decision had been made to go ahead with a new rugby competition this year. The Super Challenge Cup as it will be known will be a pool based competition run alongside the regular season with games being played on certain Saturdays during the year. Each team who joins the competition will be placed into a pool with four other teams. Only the team with the most points from each pool will advance into the finals of the competition. Every club, university or school in the region is urged to register for the competition. It will be the first time for the schoolboy age groups that private schools will play against regular club sides which should make for some entertaining rugby. This competition will finally decide who the best teams in the region are once and for all.

Rer
foll
imp

The
that
rela
the
beh
of a
exp
in h
its
beh
con
or v

It w

New Competition

Bootsie's seven weeks holiday was soon drawing to a close and he had enjoyed his time at home thoroughly. He had spent some of it catching up with Robbie and had even joined his touch rugby team again on Monday nights. There was also another player who was in the team again and it was Dan. If Bootsie thought his last year had been tough, then Dan's had been a nightmare. The difference was that Dan had brought a lot of what had happened to him onto himself, whereas Bootsie had been an innocent victim.

"I knew that car was stolen, but I didn't have the courage to just get out when I should have," Dan admitted to Bootsie and Robbie. "I thought they were cool kids and that they would have thought I was weak if I had said driving in a stolen car was dumb. Look where trying to be cool led me, straight into a reform home," added Dan.

He had spent close to 8 months inside a boys reform home and hated every second of it.

"I trained every day in that place," said Dan to the boys. "If it wasn't for boxing, then I don't know what would have happened to me. Now that I'm out though, I'm changing my life for the better. I've been given a gift on the end of each arm and I'm going to use my gift to make it in life. The worse part was looking at my dad when I was sent away. He said it broke his heart, and although I can't change the past, I can certainly do something about the future. I fully intend to make my dad proud of me again and I'm not stopping until I've got a world championship belt around my waist," added Dan. Bootsie told Dan about what had happened to him at All Kings the previous year and Dan was shocked to hear Bootsie's story.

Bootsie agreed with Dan that they had a similar outlook on life and even though they liked different sports they were both chasing the same goal, to be the best at their chosen sport. With only a week to go in his holidays, Bootsie said goodbye to Dan that night and wished him luck in reaching his goal.

"Don't worry about me, just focus on getting that test jumper?" he said to Bootsie.

"Hey, likewise. When they're hanging that belt around your waist just remember how far you came," replied Bootsie, "It'll make it even sweeter," he added. The boys said their final goodbyes and wished each other the best.

Bootsie sat down on the couch with his dad and told him about what Dan had said about the stolen car and the boys home. They both agreed that it would be a good lesson for Dan and he would be stupid if he did anything like that again.

"I think he's on the right track again," said Bootsie.

"I hope for his sake he is," replied his dad. "Must have been a huge worry for his parents," he added.

"Well Dad, all you have to worry about with me is where I'm going to put all the money I make when I'm a test superstar," replied Bootsie. Bootsie's dad laughed.

"Good to see you're so modest about it as well," replied his dad in a very sarcastic voice. "Bootsie I don't want to sound like I'm being negative, but just in case it doesn't work out, have you thought about what you might like to do?" his dad asked.

"Yeah I've got a backup plan, probably finance or engineering. I'll go to university and get a degree in either one, just in case. My coach told me that most of the test players have done something like that as a sideline just in case. Even *he's* got a degree in engineering, although the day he got it was the day he got his first test call-up and never needed to use it. But he did say I'd be an idiot if I didn't get something behind me," replied Bootsie.

"That's good. I'm glad you've thought about it," his dad added.

As the seasons change so can the sports played in each country. What can fill the sports pages of a paper for months soon gives way to other sports when that season ends. For rugby this was very true and while it wasn't filling the back page of every paper at the moment there were some very small articles starting to appear in the sports section of the papers again. One morning whilst he flicked through the sports section of the paper Bootsie noticed a small article that immediately grabbed his attention. The small headline above the article read,

Rugby's Challenge Cup is On

The regional rugby board last night announced that the decision had been made to go ahead with a new rugby competition this year. The Super Challenge Cup, as it will be known, will be a pool-based competition run alongside the regular season, with games being played on certain Saturdays during the year. Each team that joins the competition will be placed into a pool with four other teams. Only the team with the most points from each pool will advance into the finals of the competition. Every club, university or school in the region is urged to register for the competition. It will be the first time that schoolboy teams from private schools will play against regular club sides, which should make for some entertaining rugby. This competition will finally decide who the best teams in the region are once and for all!

"That's interesting," Bootsie said to his dad after reading the article, "I wonder if the headmaster at All Kings has read this? It would be great to see how we'd go against some of the club sides that I've never played against before," he added.

"What is it?" his dad asked.

"A new competition the rugby board is running this year. It's a competition where every club, university and school can put a team in, to see who the best is. Imagine All Kings against the Central Cobras, or the Sharks. It would be great," he added.

"What about All Kings against the Hornets, had you thought of that?" replied his dad with raised eyebrows.

"Oh, I hope our headmaster puts us in this competition, imagine if we play the Hornets, Robbie will finally get a taste of what private schoolboy rugby is like," Bootsie said excitedly, as he began to read the article again. Last week he wasn't ready for his holidays to end; now he couldn't wait.

3

The All Kin

Thursday Edition

WE'RE IN!!

We at the All Kings Gazette were last night informed by our magnificent headmaster that he had entered both the junior and senior boys teams in the upcoming Super Challenge Cup Competition. It is great news for the school as we finally get to display our talents against many of the regions finest school aged teams. Stay tuned to the Gazette for more information on this exciting competition. We will let you know as soon as we know what pool we have been selected in and who our first up opponents are.

Ren
foll
imp

The
that
rela
the
beh
of a
expi

A Fresh Start

The grounds of All Kings had never looked greener or better than when Bootsie and his parents arrived early on Sunday afternoon before the beginning of the new school year. Bootsie thought back to how he'd felt on this day last year. He had very different feelings this time around. Although it had been a smoother ride in the second half of last year he still had some nerves about what this year would have in store for him. "Good to be back, is it?" his dad asked him as he reached into the boot of the car for Bootsie's suitcase and bags.

"Yeah, I've got a good feeling about this year," he replied. He said goodbye to his mum again and told her he'd make sure he wrote more letters to her this year. His dad helped him carry his bags to his dormitory. It wasn't long before Bootsie found his name on a wall next to his new cubicle and he said goodbye to his dad. He began to unpack his belongings and settle back into life at All Kings, but this time it was as a senior.

He was very pleased when he found out that Syd was back from his year of travelling around the country in his caravan with his wife. Some of the new boys would soon be getting a harsh introduction to life as boarders when Syd started his first day back the following morning.

Bootsie's new dormitory supervisor was Mr Kennedy; he was a very friendly man and ran the senior dorms very differently, he just let the boys call him Kev. The senior boys were expected to understand how to behave in a dormitory environment by now and the strict discipline that was enforced on them as junior boys no longer applied, and it made for a much more relaxed time in Bootsie's new dormitory. He spent the rest of the afternoon in his cubicle listening to music before taking a stroll down to the junior boys dormitory to see if the new boarders were settling in okay. He spoke to one boy who he could see was having a hard time adjusting when his parents left him. The boy was quite upset and Bootsie spent time with him and assured him he would just have to give it time and it would get a lot easier. When he felt the boy was okay, he made his way to the dungeon for a punishing weights session. He had used his weights at home every day but the much better equipment at All Kings left him feeling very sore.

He caught up with his old friend Razzi who once again began bouncing around like a wound up toy when he saw Bootsie.

"What happened to you?" he asked

Bootsie when he stopped trying to wrestle his old friend into a headlock. "What do you mean?" asked Bootsie as he straightened his messed up T-shirt, all thanks to an over excited Razzi.

"You got so tall," said Razzi.

"Oh yeah, it happened over the holidays. My body was aching for weeks so my mum took me to the doctor and he said it was probably a growth spurt. What about you Razzi, you must be nearly 5 foot now?" Bootsie asked with a smile, as he rubbed Razzi on his head.

"5 feet 7 inches and all muscle," replied Razzi, as he swatted Bootsie's hand away from his carefully styled hair. "Don't touch the hair," he added as he checked himself in Bootsie's mirror.

"Get the clippers out," Bootsie said, as he grabbed Razzi in a headlock and imitated the noise of hair clippers.

"What, and end up looking like you? No way, never," replied Razzi as he was released from Bootsie's strong grip. "Did you hear about the new competition this year?" Razzi asked Bootsie.

"Yeah I read about it, sounds pretty good," he replied as he took a seat on his bed. "Hopefully the headmaster will go for it," he added.

"Are you kidding? If there's a trophy up for grabs, we'll be in it," replied Razzi, as he sat down next to Bootsie.

Everyone at All Kings knows when it's getting close to rugby season because any non-rugby stories in the press come to a grinding halt and are replaced with stories about the teams and players, no matter how trivial they might be. Last year's incident with Bootsie had really given them something to get their teeth into and for some reason not a single copy of those editions ever made there way into Bootsie's hands, funny that. The first front-cover rugby story of the season had the headline WE'RE IN! It covered the headmaster's decision to enter All Kings in the Super Challenge Cup competition. Bootsie was very pleased when he read the article and wasn't surprised when it went on to say how many teams had registered for the competition. It was a bold move by the regional rugby board to try this new competition, but judging by the positive response it had received from clubs wanting to participate, it had made the right decision.

"Sounds like it could be a good competition, I wonder who will be in our pool," he thought to himself after reading the article. Bootsie discussed the Super Challenge Cup with the coach one afternoon when he saw him walking through the school grounds.

"What do you think of the competition?" Bootsie asked his coach.
"Depends how you see it I suppose.
The season is stretched longer now
and it means teams will be playing
extra games a season. Injuries can
hamper a team with the number
of games teams play now, let alone
adding more games to the tally. It's
amazing what money will do, but I
can see for some of the club sides out
there, who are financially struggling,
that the prize money could really help
them out, which really isn't a concern
here," he replied to Bootsie.
"So why are we in it then? Not that
I'm complaining," asked Bootsie.
"The trophy and the right to say we're
number 1. The old boy really loves
this place and he feels like his own
reputation took a beating along with
the good name of the school with
that incident last year. I don't know

about you Bootsie, but if winning this thing can win back something for this school's reputation, then I'm all for it," the coach said to Bootsie.

Bootsie stood and thought about what he had just heard; even *he* didn't know how hard the headmaster had taken the incident and the negative press that came with it. He vowed to the coach he would do whatever it took to help win that Cup.

4

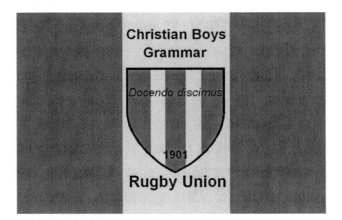

Bonus Points

The coach at All Kings had a very steady approach to pre-season training at the school. It was very different to that of the Charlton Hall coach who had been bent on breaking his troops into machines, not rugby players. When Bootsie thought back as to how bad the training had been at Charlton Hall, it was probably the best thing that could have happened when the coach stood down from the role. In a letter he had received from Charlie, Bootsie learnt that the coach had been given a coaching role at another school and Charlie said it was one of the greatest moments in his young life when Charlton Hall punished the old coaches' new team, when they played recently.

The coach at All Kings was very well respected by his players and it wasn't out of fear of his enormous frame either, it was due to his ability to connect with all his players. He knew each boy had a different personality and he treated them accordingly. He would use different methods to train and encourage them and it worked very effectively. Both the junior and senior teams were in great shape before the first round of the season and were ready to take on all comers including any teams they hadn't heard of that were registered to play in the Super Challenge Cup games.

On the first night of pre-season training, Bootsie asked his coach if he thought he should play at number 8 for the rest of his career and really focus on making it his specialty position.

"What do you think coach, should I stick to the back of the scrum?" he asked him.

"Actually Bootsie, I think you should move further into it," he replied.

"What do you mean by that?" asked Bootsie with a slightly confused look on his face.

"I think with your height and size we should start looking at second row for you this year Bootsie," replied the coach.

"What about number 8?" asked Bootsie.

"You're going to grow a few more inches yet, which will make you the perfect height for a lock forward, I think that's the position you should be training for," he replied.

"But I've never played second row," said Bootsie.

"Look Bootsie, if I didn't think it was a good idea I wouldn't have suggested it," he said to Bootsie. "Besides you've got me here to teach you the finer points of being a good lock," he added. Bootsie agreed to try what his coach had suggested and start training as a lock forward, besides who was *he* to argue with an ex-test, second-row legend like his coach. If anyone knew about that position, then it was him.

Pre-season training soon gave way for the first game of the regular season and All Kings were up against Christian Boys Grammar. Being on the senior boys team now, meant he got to watch the first half of the junior game each week. Their fly half who was now the captain of the junior boys was an absolute sensation in the role. His name was Joey and he was born to play rugby. Bootsie's coach had put Joey down for his scholarship selection and he was picked by the headmaster to be last year's sports scholarship choice, just like Bootsie had been when he first came to All Kings. He was a great playmaker for the junior boys and by half time they were ahead again. All Kings 21, Christian Boys 3.

Bootsie wished some of the junior boys well, as they ran out of the changing rooms after half time, then he went in to change for his game. This was his first game as a lock forward or second rower as some people call it. He didn't think it was too much different from being number 8 but being in the tight five meant he couldn't break off the back of the scrum, which he'd always liked doing in the past. He was getting used to being lifted in the lineouts at training and enjoyed being lifted a lot more than being one of the lifters. Their lineouts weren't the best yet, but with some extra training Bootsie knew his forwards would soon be getting it right. His starting partner in the second row was also a big unit and his name was Ash, he was also a fifth former and had played second row for most of his time at All Kings. At training the lineouts hadn't been perfect, but as Bootsie laced up his boots he just hoped that today it worked.

The winning junior boys team made a guard of honour and clapped the senior boys onto the ground ready for their game. The junior boys team had run out convincing winners over Christian Boys junior team and the final score was All Kings 42, Christian Boys 14.

As Bootsie stood on the field he remembered back to his first game ever for All Kings and how the screaming crowd had put him off his game completely. Today's opposition was the same school he had played against on that first day and no matter how many boys were here waving red and yellow ribbons on the sideline, he knew it wasn't going to affect him. Over all the screaming from the sidelines he barely heard the whistle and the game was underway.

Playing in the second row meant it was still his job to bash into the rucks which Bootsie loved doing. It was also one of his jobs to be given the ball at the back of a ruck and made to charge at the opposition's defensive line. If he took the ball at a lineout and a maul formed around him, he would be urging his forward pack to push as hard as they could and drive the ball upfield towards the goal line. For the first game of the year the All Kings senior boys were really putting it together well, or so they thought. Most of the team were fifth formers and had played together in the junior team and last year as fourth form bench players trying to break into the tough senior side. For any fourth formers this year they would be having a tough time breaking into this tight team, by half time the score was All Kings 12, Christian Boys 6.

"Not a bad start to the year, boys," the coach said to the group at half time. "I've seen some reasonable things already from you boys and we're only 40 minutes into the season. Okay, the lineout is terrible but that's something that we'll have to work on more. Bootsie, I want more aggression from you in the lineouts when you're jumping. Don't let me see that ball get stolen from you again. When you're in the air grab that ball and hang onto it like its gold, okay?" he said to Bootsie who was sucking water from a water bottle. "The backs are doing well but if it's a 50/50 pass then don't throw it, go to ground and wait for the support to arrive. That goes for all of you as well, if you can't see someone to offload to then hang onto it. We had some good runs at their line and it was wasted by stupid passes when no one was there to catch it. Forwards, you've got to get to the breakdowns quicker. I've seen us lose possession twice because you boys were too slow to get there. Harves if you don't stop telling the referee how to do his job then I'll replace you. You've given away two penalties because of your back chatting," he said sternly to Dan, the mouthy scrum half whose last name was Harvey but everyone called him Harves. "Now I want you to go out there and put an All Kings stamp on this game and send a message that this year is an All Kings year," he said to the boys in the most animated voice Bootsie had ever hear him use.

The boys began to notice how seriously the coach took the senior boys games. He told them that the junior boys team was all about development as a player, but by the time they were in fifth form he expected results from all the time he had spent with each of them over the years. Bootsie listened to every word that came out of his coach's mouth that day and did everything that was asked of him. He knew how good this coach had been in his day and he had to take every bit of knowledge he could away with him before he left All Kings at the end of the year.

The lineout was still a shambles, but at least Bootsie didn't get the ball ripped off him anymore in the second half. The Christian Grammar boys bounced back early in the second half and the score was soon level at 17 all. Bootsie took it upon himself to rally the troops and get the game back on track. Harves was taken off by the coach because he constantly told the referee how to do his job, so, true to his word, the coach replaced him with one of the fourth form boys who wasn't a bad halfback, at least he could keep his mouth shut, well, as much as a scrum half can anyway. With Bootsie leading the way and Harves sitting on the bench, the team lifted and came away with a narrow 3 point win. The final score was All Kings 20, Christian Grammar 17. It was a win but all the boys knew how important bonus points were in this competition and today they missed out on one. Even the losing team came away with 1 bonus point and the coach wasn't happy.

5

BOOTSIE FOR CAPTAIN

It was shown yesterday in no uncertain terms that Bootsie is the man for the job when it comes to the captaincy of the senior boy's team. He demonstrated an excellent display of leadership from the front yesterday when what looked like a strong run home from the Christian Boys Grammar team was stopped by a boy who stepped up and showed what a true leader he is. So you must all agree that without a doubt Bootsie is our man for the senior captaincy this year.

Even though they scraped home yesterday with a gutsy win against a team that wasn't expected to perform away from home it wasn't enough to secure a bonus point. Dan 'Harves' Harvey was at his mouthy best and continued to help out the referee in telling him how to do his job. His constant advice to the men in charge was enough to get him offside with the rest of the All Kings players and constantly give penalty decisions to the other side. Finally enough was enough and he was taken off much to the delight of most of the All Kings faithful.

Ren
foll
imp

The
that
rela
the
beh
of a
expr
in li
its
beh
con
or v

It m
tota
thin
dec

Captain

The morning paper that was sometimes pinned to Bootsie's wardrobe door when he awoke on Sunday mornings had now started to be left at the foot of the bed in his cubicle. After all this time at All Kings he had only just learned that if the paper was pinned to his wardrobe door it was going to be an ugly story about him or his team. Today it was obviously going to be good. He reached down and grabbed his copy of the Gazette and lay back in his bed to read what the boy journalists had come up with from their late night efforts. Most of the boy journalists were now fifth formers and boy, did they like sticking it to the juniors, the problem was they had been a fantastic team last year and judging by yesterday's efforts were going to follow the same path this year as well. Bootsie looked at the headline on the front of the paper;

it read, "BOOTSIE FOR CAPTAIN" in bold letters. "Interesting," he thought to himself as he began to read the article.

It was shown yesterday in no uncertain terms that Bootsie is the man for the job when it comes to the captaincy of the senior boys team. He demonstrated an excellent display of leadership from the front yesterday when what looked like a strong run home from the Christian Boys Grammar team was stopped by a boy who stepped up and showed what a true leader he is. So you must all agree that without a doubt Bootsie is our man for the senior captaincy this year.

"This one's getting sent home," he thought to himself as he read the rest of the article.

Even though they scraped home yesterday with a gutsy win against a team that wasn't expected to perform away from home, it wasn't enough to secure a bonus point. Dan 'Harves' Harvey was at his mouthy best and continued to help out the referee in telling him how to do his job. His constant advice to the man in charge was enough to get him offside with the rest of the All Kings players and constantly gave penalty decisions to the other side. Finally, enough was enough and he was taken off, much to the delight of most of the All Kings faithful.

Our junior boys followed on their good form from last year and led by their captain Joe had an easy win for their first game. There is

a full coverage of the junior boys'
game in the sports section of the
paper.

"Ouch! I guess Harves has got his paper pinned to his wardrobe this week," Bootsie thought to himself as he read the stinging report on his team's scrum half. He did agree that Harves had spent the game telling the referee how to do his job, and once the referee had had enough of his constant chatter, Christian Boys Grammar were getting a lot of the close decisions going their way. No referee likes a mouthy player who constantly tells him what to do and Harves was a shocker for it. As a halfback he was a sensation, but his mouth just got him into so much trouble each week. At least last year he was the reserve halfback and for most of the year only got ten minutes a game. The boys joked that he should be put in as the fullback because at least that way he's the furthest player away from the referee for most of the game. Bootsie was at Charlton Hall the year that Harves was the starting halfback each week when he was a third former in the junior team, but Razzi had told Bootsie about how many yellow cards Harves got in that season. The boys had bets each week for what minute of the game Harves would be given ten minutes to cool off on the bench from another yellow card. Bootsie knew if he was made captain he would seriously have to speak to Harves about the non-stop flapping of his gums to the referee.

At training during the week it was no surprise when Bootsie was made the captain of the senior boys team. He felt quite honoured to be given the responsibility of leading the senior boys in his final year and wanted to go out with some silverware. The next two games were disastrous for him as a captain and the boys lost to St Peter's at their home ground 21 to 6 and then the following week picked up a losing bonus point when they again lost to Saint David's at home 17 to 15. Those two weeks Bootsie woke up with a copy of the school paper pinned to his wardrobe door and he didn't like what he read. The first week's headline wasn't too bad and it read, "CAPTAIN GETS OFF TO BAD START" but this week's headline had a little more sting to it.

"CAPTAIN'S SHIP IS SINKING" was the headline that greeted Bootsie on the Sunday morning after the loss against Saint David's. Bootsie had played his heart out for that game and to read such harsh criticism the next day didn't go down well with him.

One of the boy journalist's cubicles was directly opposite Bootsie's cubicle and he couldn't help asking the boy about the article on the Sunday after breakfast. The boy turned to Bootsie and said, "Hey, we just write what we see," which didn't make Bootsie feel any better about it. Bootsie said to the boy, "If you think we're sinking then you're wrong, we may be going through a storm but we're definitely not sinking." Bootsie thought it was a pretty clever comeback, but didn't realise it would be used for a headline in the Thursday edition of the paper. When the midweek paper came out the headline read, THE SHIP ISN'T SINKING, BUT IT IS LOST IN A STORM". Bootsie thought that next time he'd say nothing and let the boy journalists come up with their own headlines, he wouldn't be giving them any more lines to work with in the future.

On Saturday as he stood on the ground waiting for the start of his game Bootsie felt the pressure of being captain for the first time. Under his captaincy he was zero wins from two starts and the senior team was third from the bottom on 5 points, this wasn't the start he was after. It didn't help that the junior boys were sitting on top of their table after 4 wins from 4 starts, they had easily accounted for both St Peter's and St David's but had just scraped home today by 6 points. Bootsie only hoped the senior boys could come away with a 6 point win today and when the ball was kicked over the touch line by the All Kings flyhalf at the kickoff it wasn't the start he was after. The scrum was set in the middle of the halfway line and before the Westchester halfback fed the ball, Harves gave away a penalty for backchat and before Bootsie knew it, they were inside their own 22 defending a lineout. The boys had practiced the lineouts over and over again at training and had got them down pretty good, but the first one they set today was awful. Bootsie jumped at two and was dropped from a great height after being pulled down by the Westchester boy who was jumping next to him. It didn't matter at all because nobody saw it, but when Bootsie looked up in a daze, he could see the Westchester boys celebrating the try they had just scored. After the conversion and with only five minutes gone on the clock the score was All Kings 0, Westchester 7.

The rest of the first half continued the same way from that point, Harves told the referee *he* could do a better job of refereeing the game and he was shown the all-familiar yellow card. Razzi then shoulder charged a Westchester player two minutes later and he was also shown the same colour card as well. Thirteen against fifteen doesn't add up on a rugby field and with two missing players there were two holes in the defensive wall. It didn't take Westchester long to take advantage of the situation and by half time the score had already blown out to an embarrassing All Kings 0, Westchester 28. As Bootsie pulled out his mouth guard and walked back to the change rooms he knew the game was all but gone and Westchester already had a 4 try bonus point.

For a calm man, the All Kings coach sure could breathe fire when he had to. Bootsie was shocked to see and hear how furious the coach was and how he held nothing back when he addressed the troops at the break. Bootsie copped a massive spray about his lack of leadership in controlling his teammates, which he didn't like at all.

Razzi and Harves were both benched for the rest of the game and two fourth formers were brought into the game to show that lack of discipline was not going to be tolerated. The coach really raised his voice for the first time and he told the team in no uncertain terms that any boy that was given a yellow card should put his tracksuit on because that was the end of his day.

The rev-up the coach gave the boys seemed to fire them up for the first five minutes of the start of the second half, but Bootsie was already reading the headlines in his head and there was no way he wanted to go down a loser again today. He smashed his big frame into any player who touched the ball or dared to run at him, the spray at half time had really annoyed him and he couldn't work out why he had copped such an ear bashing over two of his teammates' lack of discipline.

"If it's so important to win then why doesn't the coach put Harves and Razzi back on?" Bootsie thought to himself as he watched the Westchester fly half convert another try they had just scored. It was one of the worst games Bootsie had played in and he felt like he was the only one who had given anything positive out on the field. With a final score of All Kings 0, Westchester 41, he couldn't wait to read the next morning's headline.

6

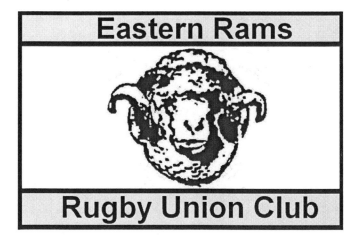

Headlines

When Bootsie was back in his cubicle after returning from Westchester College, he was asked by a boy journalist if he had any comments on the game before he went over to the gazette office. Bootsie tried to be as professional as he could about the game and said to the boy, "We need to make some changes." After writing what Bootsie had just said in a pad he kept in his top pocket, the boy left the dormitory and headed for his usual Saturday night routine at the office where the gazette was made. Bootsie spent the rest of the evening thinking about the game over and over in his head. He was disappointed in the result and couldn't remember many worse games he had played in before. He felt he had played *his* best and some of the other boys had put in some effort but as a whole the effort of the team was poor to say the least. He had copped a massive rap on the knuckles from the coach at half time and it was the first time since he had been at All Kings that he had been annoyed with his coach.

"Why did I get such a spray for the others being sent off?" he kept saying to himself over and over. This dressing down kept him up late into the night before he eventually fell asleep and awoke to find the Sunday copy of the gazette pinned to his wardrobe door. He thought he may as well look at it now and get it over with. In bold letters on the front page it said, SHIP HITS AN ICEBERG AND SINKS.

Bootsie didn't read the article. Instead, he filed the paper in the plastic filing cabinet he kept under his desk; most people know it as a bin. He went for a run before breakfast to clear his mind about the disaster that was yesterday. After the run he felt slightly better about the game and after a punishing weights session late on Sunday afternoon he felt a lot better about it. The school was abuzz on Monday morning when the draws for the Super Challenge Cup came out, it was supposed to happen the previous week but there had been a problem with the closing date for registration and more teams were now registered. Every day the region's morning paper would arrive at All Kings and on this particular morning there was a queue waiting for the five copies that the school received. It was a race between the first five boys who grabbed the papers from the delivery person to see who was first to find All Kings opponents for round one. At almost the same time, three boys shouted out, "The Rams for the senior boys and the Hornets for the junior boys.

"The Hornets?" Bootsie said out loud, as he stood listening nearby.

"Who are the Rams? And the Hornets?" one boy asked.

"I've never heard of the Rams but I definitely know the Hornets," added Bootsie.

"I don't know either of them," a boy reading one of the papers replied. Another boy soon pointed out there was a pull-out section of the paper that listed every club that would be competing, including a little information about that club.

"Here we go. The Rams..." he said as he read aloud to the group. "The Eastern Rams have a fierce reputation in their local competition and the first grade team has won the flag for the last two years running. They are considered to be in the top 20 teams for the first grade teams division, their junior sides have also followed on in similar tradition with all grades, except second grade, winning that competition's grand final game last year. The senior schoolboys' team was undefeated last year and convincingly won their grand final for the second year running. Great first round opponents," the boy added, as he finished reading the article to the group.

"What does it say about us?" another boy asked him.

"Hang on, where are we? Aah, here we are, All Kings. All Kings used to be considered one of the better schools competing in the private schoolboys' competition in their area. Despite poor performances from the senior boys team in recent years and sitting close to the bottom of the ladder, this year they will have a tough challenge ahead of them. First up opponents are the Rams for the senior team and the Northern Hornets for the junior team.

The way the first pool games worked out meant that both All Kings teams would be away from home for their first game in the competition. From reading the paper Bootsie knew the senior boys were in for the tougher of the two games. The Hornets weren't considered to be a match for the junior All Kings boys based on their recent performances, even the first grade team wasn't considered in the region's top 20 chances of making the final. It would be the first time in the history of All Kings that the two teams would be travelling to different grounds on a Saturday morning. It also divided the school into who would go and watch which game. There was a show of hands on the Friday in the dining hall as to who would be going to watch each game. Ninety nine percent of the hands raised seemed to be fair-weather fans as they voted against following the senior boys south where the forecast of thunderstorms was almost as bad as seeing the senior boys get smashed by a very successful opposition in the Rams. Most boys wanted to take the trip north, to much better weather and to cheer on the junior boys in their attempt to win their first game, which they were expected to do comfortably.

As the buses pulled out from the grounds of All Kings early on Saturday morning there was one bus heading south and four buses heading north. As Bootsie put on his headphones he could see the dark skies that the bus was heading towards. The senior boys were very quiet on the way down to the Rams' home ground and Bootsie knew his team had been harshly criticised in the paper even though he didn't read the article himself. The All Kings coach was on the bus with the senior boys and he was very quiet on the way down as well, probably thinking of the All Kings headmaster who was taking on the role of coach for the junior boys team. As the bus pulled into the grounds of the Rams home ground, Bootsie could only hope they could salvage something good this week and hopefully pull off the impossible and win.

By the time the boys had changed, the heavens had opened and it was bucketing down. The change rooms were very different to the luxury they were used to back at the school, this one was pretty much a brick shed, which leaked very badly. As they sat and listened to the address from the coach they could hear the cracks of thunder and see the sky light up through the front door when the lightning flashed.

As the boys ran out of the damp change rooms, the rain was coming down like a curtain. It was hard to run in the terrible conditions and the boys were instantly soaked through. The referee's whistle was impossible to hear over the rain, but when the ball sailed towards Bootsie he knew the game had started. Somehow he managed to hang onto the ball and charge towards the oncoming Rams defenders. The first wave of defenders were nothing like Bootsie had expected and he charged his massive frame straight through them and all he could see was a lonely fullback and a winger out to the right of him as he charged into the empty space.

The winger ran towards Bootsie and when Bootsie put his hand on his opponent's chest and pushed him over, he only had the fullback to beat. He was full of adrenaline and charged at the waiting defender. When he could see the look of fear in the defender's eyes he knew he was over. He dived over the line and heard the referee's whistle as he was awarded the try. First points to the All Kings boys.

As Bootsie stood up to greet his teammates who were jumping all over him, he snapped at them to get back to the halfway line and get ready for the restart. After the missed conversion, the first score was All Kings 5, Rams 0. For the rest of the first half Bootsie led the troops from the front, Harves and Razzi had to settle for starting on the bench and his starting fourth form scrum half had kept his mouth shut and no penalties had been given away. With the rain continually pouring down and the ball becoming very wet, the game was full of handling errors and the score at half time remained at All Kings 5, Rams 0.

The coach didn't say much to the boys at half time other than they knew what to do if they wanted any credibility back at the school. His only advice was, "If you get the ball hang onto it and charge." When the boys took to the field for the second half, the rain was even heavier and the field resembled a mud bath. It was a hard game to play in, and after their initial lapse in defence the Rams' boys tightened up and were very good. There was no way this was going to be a high scoring game and with ten minutes to go the score hadn't changed at all. The game had taken its toll and although he didn't really want to, the coach had no choice but to put Razzi and Harves on for the last ten minutes. Harves couldn't even keep his mouth shut for two minutes. The referee was soon sick of being told how to do his job, so he gave the Rams player a penalty, which he somehow managed to convert. After the successful kick, Bootsie grabbed Harves by his shirtfront and screamed at him, "Can you ever keep your mouth shut? You're going to cost us the game." The sudden outburst from Bootsie worked and for the rest of the game Harves didn't say boo. After witnessing the spray from the captain, Razzi also managed to stay clear of the referee's yellow card and when the final whistle blew, the All Kings boys had managed to scrape a two-point win against a very decent team in the Rams.

Bootsie was the first one to scream out in joy after the whistle and he was soon joined by his teammates. It had been a tough game in the rain and he knew it had been a huge achievement to come away with a win down here. There was a lot more riding on today than just making it through the first round of games, hopefully this would be the spark the team needed.

7

Survivors

The bus trip back to All Kings was a lot rowdier than the trip down south. There was only a handful of fourth form boys who were trying to crack into the senior team and one boy journalist who came along to watch the Rams game, other than that it was the 22 senior boys and the coach on the bus. Bootsie felt great about the win and the fact that the boys were into the next round of the cup in a few weeks. When he stepped off the bus, his coach took him aside and told him to wait until the other boys had gone, as he wanted to talk to him. Bootsie hung around until it was only himself and the coach left standing beside the parked buses.

"Learn anything in the last week?" he asked Bootsie.
"I think today I learned a lot," he replied.

"Yeah like what?" he asked Bootsie, not happy with his answer.

"About being a captain. I couldn't understand why you gave me such a spray last week at half time, but today it became a lot clearer. I realised today that you can't be friends with everyone if you want to put the team first. If Harves hates me for my outburst I can't help him, I had to do it for the team," replied Bootsie.

"Finally you see it," he said to Bootsie with a smile.

"What do you mean?" Bootsie replied.

"To be a good captain or even a coach, sometimes you've got to tell it like it is. In the last few weeks you've been too scared to stand up and be a proper captain because *you* were afraid that you might upset your teammates. If they don't like you for telling them when *they* have done something stupid, then it's too bad for them.

If they drop the ball or make a bad decision and you yell at them, then you're the idiot and the team will soon lose respect for you, but it's your job to keep control over the discipline of the team and today you showed what a real captain you can be," he replied to Bootsie.

At the supper table that evening Bootsie was approached by one of the junior rugby players.

"I'm glad at least one of us won a game today," he said.

"Yeah, and I heard you guys got quite a touch up against the Hornets," replied Bootsie.

"We sure did. And to make it worse, Joe our halfback was taken to hospital. He really hurt his arm bad," added the junior boy who was looking a little sorry for himself. Bootsie put his hand on the younger player's shoulder and said, "Look rugby's a bit like life, some days you win and some days...well let's just say you come second, and you can certainly learn a lot from coming second sometimes. The important thing is to never give up, keep pushing forward and good things will come to you. I'll try and catch up with Joe as well this week to see if he's okay." The boy looked up at Bootsie, smiled and said, "Wow, I heard you were a great captain, now I can see what they meant."

When Bootsie woke the next morning, he thought about his conversation with his coach the night before. It suddenly became clear to him why *he* was the target for the spray the previous week more than Harves and Razzi. He should have pulled them aside after their warning from the referee, but he didn't, because as the coach had pointed out, Bootsie didn't want the boys to be angry with him.

After the game Harves had apologised to Bootsie. He'd soon realised that the team had slogged their guts out in the wet for 70 minutes, and after he was on for only two minutes he nearly cost them the game. It was lucky the Rams' captain had a brain snap and chose to go for the posts, possibly thinking they had more time left than they did. The All Kings boys came away with the win and the rest as they say is history.

As he had hoped, the school paper was sitting on his bed that morning and when he looked at the headlines it was quite good, in bold letters it read, SURVIVORS FOUND AFTER SHIP SINKS. He lay back and read the article.

After losing almost all hope this year, the senior boys managed to pull off a sensational victory yesterday in appalling conditions when they travelled south to play the Eastern Rams at their home ground. As this journalist who travelled to the ground and stood on the sidelines in the terrible conditions can confirm, the senior boys played their hearts out. From the opening play of the game, the senior boys captain Bootsie was over the try line inside a minute. What looked like may be an easy victory soon became a very tough game in flooding rain, when the Rams defence suddenly tightened up after an initial lapse. The score remained at All Kings 5, Rams 0 for the entire game, until once again Harves gave away a penalty after only being allowed on in the last ten minutes due to his normal mouthy comments to the referee. For some reason the Rams captain chose the posts and the score was a nail biting 5 to 3 with minutes to go. For the first time since he was appointed captain, Bootsie stood up and took control of his team, when he was seen to grab his halfback by his shirtfront and in no uncertain terms tell him to keep his mouth shut and his opinion of the referee's decision to himself. The boys managed to stay penalty free for the last five minutes and hung on for a very hard-fought victory. In what was one of the gutsiest performances I've ever seen, they are to be congratulated on their win and first points in the competition.

Our junior boys came back with a different story. There is a full wrap-up of their game in the sports section of the paper.

"That's a bit nicer," Bootsie thought to himself, after reading the article.

At training during the week he didn't know what to expect from his teammates when he arrived. He certainly wasn't expecting the positive response he got when he arrived there; he was expecting a backlash but instead got a great reception. Bootsie was asked by his coach to address the group of senior boys before their training got under way.

"What do you want me to say?" he asked his coach quietly and away from the other boys.

"Whatever you think you need to. It's your team," he replied. Bootsie started by thanking them for their commitment and hard work in the game against the Rams. He went on to explain that lack of discipline had cost them dearly this year and it was to stop from now on. He didn't single anyone out but let them all know how poor discipline could have cost them a lot more than the game last week. He also told the group that any more yellow cards would result in the player being dropped from the starting 15 for the following week. The boys seemed to respond positively to the talk except for the last thing he said. He received a few groans when he told the group that on the days they didn't train, they were to meet in the dungeon for weights straight after the day's classes and only Sunday would be a rest day. The boys all agreed and Bootsie told the group this was going to be the turning point of the season for the team.

Did it work? You bet it worked. After a blistering training session the boys followed it up with a crushing win over St Benedict's on the Saturday at St Benedict's home ground. A week later, the boys continued their comeback with a win at home over a very poor St Peter's side. They smashed the opposition's forward pack that day and the final score was All Kings 70, St Peter's 5. There was a new spirit in the senior boys team after consecutive wins in the normal season on top of their good win over the Rams a few weeks ago.

Whether it was something in the water at All Kings recently, or just a run of bad luck, the junior boys were having a tough time of it. The junior boys' fly half sensation Joe was out for the rest of the season with a broken arm and since the team's loss against the Hornets they were unable to get a win on the board in the regular season games.

Bootsie awoke each Sunday morning to a paper sitting on his bed with headlines about the poor performance of the junior boys team; it was a relief to lose the sinking ship headlines that the senior boys had faced earlier in the season.

With all the excitement about the Super Challenge Cup game coming up again and the winning and losing forms of the teams, it could have been easy to overlook one of the most important events of the year; the trip away. Even Bootsie knew it was coming this week but had been solely focused on the new competition and the winning ways of the senior boys team. What a turnaround their season had taken. Harves learned to keep his comments about the referee quiet after the headmaster arranged for him to referee an under 13's game in the area's normal club competition. With the young halfback on one of the teams constantly telling Harves every decision he made was wrong, he soon learned what it must be like for a referee listening to him every week. He came back from that game with a whole new attitude. He was focused on playing the game each week and no longer worried about what the referee was doing. He became a try scoring machine.

The morning after the St Peter's game was the first day of the school holidays and the boys were heading off for a 10-day tour to another overseas destination chosen by the headmaster's secretary and her accurate dart throw. What a start the season had taken on, the boys had gone from nearly the lowest point on the ladder to climbing their way into a decent position at the halfway point of the season. Bootsie lay in bed that night and thought about the 10-day holiday in front of him. For the first time this year he was pleased with his decision to return to All Kings and couldn't wait for his first overseas rugby trip with All Kings to begin.

8

The Tour

When Bootsie awoke early on Sunday morning there was something different hanging on his wardrobe door and it was much nicer than a copy of the All Kings gazette. He jumped out of bed and looked at the brand new All Kings blazer, which was lit up by the morning sunshine that was streaming through the dormitory window. It was still black with the same green and yellow striping of a normal school blazer but this one had a special logo on the top pocket. It said, 'All Kings Rugby Tour', 'Senior Team Captain', followed by the name of the country they were visiting and the date of the tour embroidered below. Being a member of the rugby team could be very hard in the goldfish bowl environment of All Kings, but when Bootsie got dressed and put on his new touring blazer he thought it was well worth it.

As he sat at the breakfast table with all the other boys who had been given a new blazer, he looked around and felt very proud of where he was sitting. Two boys at another table and wearing the new blazer were boy journalists who were going with them on the tour. Mr Wood had also been chosen to go on the trip and was looking very happy to be wearing the new blazer and sitting next to the coach at the teachers' table in the dining hall.

After a rushed breakfast the boys who were going on the tour were whisked onto the buses for the short trip to the airport. This year for the first time only the senior boys were going on tour as the schools they would be staying at could only accommodate a maximum of 30 extra visitors. The junior boys would have to wait for another two years to get their turn to go again, and even the headmaster was staying back this year.

The boys all groaned as they were told one more time about what was expected of them when they were away from the school, especially due to the fact that they had 'All Kings' written on their blazers and the school had had enough bad press lately. They were warned that any misbehaviour would result in a quick flight back to All Kings followed by suspension or worse, expulsion. As soon as they arrived at the airport the boys were quickly checked in and soon after were on a flight heading overseas.

With the time difference between the two countries the boys didn't know what time it was when they arrived at their destination. They were exhausted from the early morning start and the long flight and all they cared about was a bed. After going through the various formalities and collecting their luggage, they exited the airport and boarded a waiting coach. The drive to their first host school was long, but at last they arrived, and after a late supper were shown to the guest dormitory. Mr Wood and the coach had no arguments from the boys about going straight to bed.

The next morning they were given a tour of St George's College for Boys in freezing wintery conditions. The grounds of the school were absolutely beautiful and with a background of snow-capped mountains and beautiful cherry blossom trees in full bloom everywhere it was certainly a very pretty place to stay. For the next few days the boys were driven around to different places on the same coach that picked them up from the airport, and it gave Bootsie and the rest of the boys a taste of what it must be like to be a test player on tour for his country. Wherever they visited they were always introduced in the national language, but the words 'All Kings' and 'rugby union' were the only bits the boys understood just before people would start clapping them. Bootsie had no idea what else had just been said about them.

A strange thing for the All Kings boys was that they were going to play two games against two of the country's top rugby schools and they would both be played on Wednesday afternoons. Amazingly both of the school teams were still going to play in their regular season games on the Saturdays. The boys were treated very well by their host school and Bootsie had never been so well fed before, they were always invited to go up and get their meals first and the food was plentiful. Judging by how big some of the boys in the St George's team were, Bootsie guessed that the amount of food at each meal was always like this.

On the Wednesday afternoon the sidelines of the school's rugby field were filled with boys waving red and white ribbons. It was a huge school and by the time the game started the sidelines were packed. Although the air was cold the sun was shining and it was Bootsie's first game on tour playing for All Kings, instead of playing against them like the previous time. The whistle was blown and the game was on.

The St George's boys were certainly out to play even if it was a Wednesday afternoon; and they were good too, not at all what Bootsie was expecting. The senior boys' front row was having awful trouble with the massive front row boys from St George's, in fact the whole scrum was having a terrible time and Bootsie was in the middle of it. He was comfortable now in the second row and he loved pushing against the props and hooker and driving the scrum along. Each time a scrum packed down, the heat that poured out from the players' bodies hit the cold air and it looked like two steam-powered locomotives had collided with each other. The game was a far more bruising encounter than Bootsie was ready for, and the host team was in front at half time. All Kings 10, St George's 17.

During the break the coach told the boys to relax and enjoy their rugby, as they weren't under the usual pressures, these trips were more about good will than winning. That was all he said, so the boys just sat back and rested before taking to the field again for the second half.

The boys did relax when they started the second half and they relaxed a little too much because before they knew it the host boys drove a maul over the try line and after the conversion the score was All Kings 10, St George's 24. The coach wasn't too concerned about the win but Bootsie was, he was very competitive and couldn't see the point in playing if you weren't going to win. He took it upon himself to change the scoreline back in All Kings favour and not long after the St George's boys had scored, he barged over for his first try of the tour. He even took his own kick which he easily converted; the score was a more respectable All Kings 17, St George's 24. The rest of the game was very much the same with both teams trying their best to break each others defensive line. With only minutes to go Bootsie took the ball off the back of a ruck and after palming off two St George's defenders dived over the line for his second. He looked up to see Razzi and one of the St George's boys holding each other by their shirtfronts and glaring at each other menacingly. With the two different languages neither boy could understand what the other one was saying and it was probably just as well. Bootsie separated Razzi and the other boy and this time let Freddy the fullback take the kick, as he was better than the team's flyhalf at taking kicks from near the touchline. It was a perfect kick and it tied the game up at 24 all, and that was how the score stayed until the referee blew the whistle to end the game. The boys thought it was a fair result with both teams having given it everything they had.

The boys exchanged jumpers with the St George's boys on the field after the game as is tradition on these tours. Later in the evening after dinner Bootsie and Razzi were both asked up on stage in the dining hall and were each given another St George's rugby jumper by the school's headmaster, but these ones had the normal school logo. They both shook hands with the principal, and smiled and nodded a lot to his questions. They had no idea what he was asking, but the joke was on them when they were told by the translator that they had just agreed to play for St George's College in Saturday's game against the school's biggest rivals, The Hill Military Academy. Bootsie looked at Razzi and said, "Oops," to which Razzi said nothing and shook his head in disbelief. It was a good joke that night, but when Bootsie woke the next morning he wondered how he could play another game in two more days. The cold, hard ground had left him very sore from yesterday's game. The winter here was a lot colder than the ones he was used to at home.

One of the things Bootsie liked best were the hot baths they had at the school, and he soaked in them for ages over the next two days in an attempt to fix his aching muscles. It had been arranged that Bootsie and Razzi would play for the school in the Saturday game but they could only play in the second half, which was fine by the two boys who were still very sore. What they weren't told was that The Hill Military Academy was the best team in their competition. When the St George's boys took to the field, Bootsie and Razzi knew they had made a bad decision in saying yes to this after such a short break. As they sat on the sidelines shivering, they noticed how hard the hits were, this game was a whole level above the Wednesday game. They found out later that most of the boys in the Wednesday game weren't starting 15 players, but by playing against All Kings it gave them a chance to play in the starting 15 for the school. Bootsie and Razzi both came on early in the second half and played their part in a very brutal game between two schools that didn't like each other at all. Razzi nearly had his head taken off from a high tackle and Bootsie thought his teammate was dead from the way he was lying on the ground after the tackle. Unfortunately for their host school, Bootsie and a now very groggy Razzi couldn't help them to a win and the final score was St George's 15, The Hill Military Academy 21.

The boys spent the next few days recovering from the two games and Razzi wasn't sure what had happened to him when he woke up the next morning, he felt like he had been hit by a car. The following Wednesday Razzi opted out of the game against their new host school St Xavier's and let one of the other boys on the tour get a start in the first 15. Bootsie ran on again, easily beating the much weaker team and soon found out they hadn't won a game in two years. St Xavier was a fantastic host school and overall the entire trip had been incredible. Bootsie was especially pleased with the two new jumpers he had collected on the trip. All of the boys had enjoyed the 10-day trip and didn't want it to end yet, but the following morning they would be saying goodbye and flying back to All Kings. For some reason that night it suddenly dawned on Bootsie that this was his last year at his beloved school and pretty soon all this was going to be a memory for him. The thought of this really played on his mind and he had a hard time drifting off to sleep.

9

Familiar
Surroundings

By the time the boys arrived back at All Kings on the Friday, they didn't know where they were, they had left one time zone one day and either gained a day or lost a day but whatever had happened, by the time they arrived back at the school they were shattered. Bootsie didn't bother to unpack. He fell onto his bed and it was lights out. When he eventually awoke from his slumber he felt like a train was running through his head, he couldn't work out what all the hype at the school was about until he was eventually told it was Saturday and the boys had an away game at St Luke's. When he told one of the boy journalists to go away and not bother him again as he wasn't playing today, the boy journalist sought out the coach to ask if it was true. Bootsie soon had a large man standing at the end of his bed.

"Get up. We've got a game today," he said as he gave Bootsie's bed a kick. "I can't, I'm exhausted," replied Bootsie. "If you think you can be a test player then you'd better get used to this lifestyle," he added as he kicked the bed again. Bootsie dragged himself out of bed. "Okay, I'm up. Just stop kicking the bed," he said to the coach. As he sat on the side of his bed still trying to make sense of the new day, Bootsie couldn't think straight at all. "I'll see you in the dining hall," his coach said to him as he left for his own breakfast.

Although he hadn't toured as a test player for many years, the coach was much better at the hectic lifestyle that test players were put under. Sure he had missed his morning shave but at least he didn't resemble a walking zombie when he entered the dining hall that morning as most of the senior boys did. After breakfast Bootsie still felt like going back to bed but he knew that if he lay down again he would never get up. He headed for the showers and let the hot water pour over him as he hung onto the showerhead above him. He wasn't sure if at one stage he fell asleep as he stood there, because when the water eventually turned cold it was a sudden snap back into the world of the living. He dressed quickly and grabbed his rugby bag that he still hadn't unpacked from the trip. He knew everything he needed was in there and if his boots were mouldy he might be better leaving them that way rather than washing them in any toilet sinks again. He dragged himself onto the bus, sat down, leaned his head against the window and went back to the land of nod again.

"Hey, wake up sleepy head," a voice in Bootsie's dream said.

"Huh, what?" he said as he tried to work out why he was at home on holidays and the coach was kicking his bed.

"Bootsie wake up!" Bootsie opened his eyes and tried to focus on the world outside.

"C'mon we're here, let's go," the coach said to him, as Bootsie realised he was at St Luke's and was the only one still on the bus. He pulled his face from the dribble he had left on the window, wiped his face and staggered off the bus to join the other players. He slowly walked down the path and followed his teammates into the change rooms, found a space on a bench, then sat down to get changed. He certainly wasn't the only one feeling the effects of the last two weeks, and out on the field it showed. St Luke's weren't the best of teams in the competition and today they nearly gave All Kings a shock loss. Even as exhausted as he was, Bootsie dug deep from somewhere and ended up scoring a try for the team. He had played four tough games in the space of two weeks and he was feeling every minute of it. The All Kings boys won the game by one point and the final score was All Kings 8, St Luke's 7. After the game the coach addressed the boys in the changing rooms and was very happy that they came away with a win despite the long and tiring trip they had been on. He looked directly at Bootsie when he said that any boys who wanted to play at a test level would have to get used to feeling like this.

Bootsie spent the whole of Sunday asleep and only got up for breakfast, lunch, the evening meal and supper. He quickly browsed the school's paper at supper on Sunday night and the headline was about the junior boys' loss the previous day. There was a good full-page article about the tour and it had some great pictures of Bootsie in action. Later, he asked the boy journalist who was in the cubicle opposite him if he could have some extra copies to send home to his parents.

By the beginning of the new school week Bootsie felt a bit better despite now being forced to do extra study hours on Wednesday evenings for the impending end of year exams. He walked to the dining hall and could see a group of boys gathered around each other and hotly discussing something. As he walked up the steps into the hall a boy shouted to him, "Hey Bootsie, we've got the Bulldogs this week." It didn't register until Bootsie sat down with a bowl of cereal in front of him.

"The Bulldogs?" he said out loud, as he got up and took off outside towards the group of boys again. "Let me see," he said, as he used his imposing frame to get closer to the papers. He saw that the pools for the Super Challenge Cup had been finalised.

"All Kings versus the south's Bulldogs," he read out loud. "Yes, they're in our pool," he added with a huge smile.

"Who are the south's Bulldogs?" another boy asked Bootsie.

"That's my old team from when I was really young," he replied. "And we're away there this week," he added with an even bigger smile.

From the moment he heard the news about the Bulldogs game, he had a whole new spring in his step and he couldn't wait for Saturday to come. While most of the other boys complained about another away game, Bootsie couldn't wait to get back to the familiar surroundings of the south's Bulldogs ground. He had only played one game down there and although that wasn't overly successful he still couldn't wait to play there again. Unfortunately though, the excitement of the upcoming game made Bootsie spend most of his extra study time daydreaming. His memories of being a very young player with the Bulldogs were not going to help him come exam time.

Saturday came around at last and the team was on its way. Once they arrived in town, Bootsie directed the bus driver on the shortest way to get to the ground. This week he was the first one off the bus. As the other boys slowly got changed Bootsie was already ready and went looking for some familiar faces.

It didn't take him long before he bumped into Stinkey Taylor.

"Boo!" Bootsie said to him as he approached him. Bootsie was horrified when Stinkey cringed with a look of fear on his face at the large unit of a boy who now stood over him.

"Whatever I did, I'm sorry," Stinkey said, looking like a rabbit in the headlights of an oncoming car.

"Stinkey it's me, Bootsie," Bootsie replied.

"It is? I mean yeah, I knew that," said Stinkey, looking a lot more relaxed.

"No you didn't. Did you think I was going to hit you or something?" Bootsie asked.

"No, I just didn't recognise you any more Bootsie. You're huge," he replied. "When did you get so big?"

"I don't know. Over the last few years I suppose," replied Bootsie. Stinkey looked at Bootsie's jumper and the look of fear returned again. "What's wrong Stinkey?" Bootsie asked, knowing that something wasn't right. "All Kings, y, y, you've got All Kings written on your jumper," he replied. "Well yeah, I *do* go there, and we are playing each other today you know," said Bootsie.

"You mean I'm...I mean we're playing against your team?" asked Stinkey, looking very pale again.

"Yeah," replied Bootsie.

"Well, are they all as big as you?" asked Stinkey.

"Oh, no way!" replied Bootsie.

"Oh thank goodness for that!" added Stinkey.

"I'm only the scrum half. You should see how big our forwards are," Bootsie said, with a smile from ear to ear. Stinkey turned a funny shade of pale green before only what can be described as "Plplplplfffff" came out of him. Bootsie began waving his arms like he was being attacked by a swarm of bees.

"Oh Stinkey, that's disgusting," he said, as he took off backwards trying to get away from the awful smell that Stinkey had created. "I'll see you out there," Bootsie added, as he went back to the changing rooms.

When Bootsie took to the field with the rest of the All Kings boys, he was quite shocked as to how many of the boys on the Bulldogs team were unknown to him. He had been away for quite a while and the team had changed considerably in that time, even the club's jumpers were different now. They were still green, red and white but very different from the original ones that Bootsie had worn. When the game started and Bootsie charged after the kick, he felt no strange feelings at all about playing against his old team. When he smashed into the first defender he caught up to, who was holding the ball, he felt like he had never played for them. For the rest of the game Bootsie wanted nothing more than to go home with a win. The south's Bulldogs had won their last pool match in the previous round, but it was a huge task for them to beat a team like All Kings, especially with the rampaging Bootsie on the team. By half time All Kings were in front and the score was All Kings 35, Bulldogs 0.

The hiding continued in the second half and all the players on the bench were put on for some valuable game time at some point. Even with the reserve players on the field for most of the second half, the score blew out to an embarrassing All Kings 80, Bulldogs 0. Bootsie shook hands with all the Bulldogs players and Stinkey was the only one he knew. "Where is everyone?" he asked Stinkey after the game.

"Don't know. Some have moved town and some don't want to play any more I suppose," he replied.

"What about Sione, Sunnie, Ali, Tua and Ben?" Bootsie asked.

"Same thing. The Island connection moved houses and play for the Cats now, and Ben moved away last year, somewhere," Stinkey replied. Before Bootsie could ask any more questions he could feel someone standing behind him. He heard a large, deep voice say, "Look at the size of you boy!"

"Coach Van Den?" Bootsie said, as he turned around. "My goodness it *is* you," he replied. Bootsie spent the next half hour talking to his old coach before being told to get ready, as the bus was about to leave.

"Bootsie, if I don't say this now I may never get the chance later. From the first day I met you, I always thought you had the ability and the attitude to play for your country one day.

There was always something special about you and after seeing you play today and the way you're going I don't think it's going to be too far away for you now," said coach Van Den with a smile, just before Bootsie turned and boarded the bus. Bootsie sat on the bus in a stunned silence, Coach Van Den's praise for him really had an impact and it made him even more determined to fulfill his dream of a test spot.

10

Just One More

Over the next five rounds the action in the Private Schoolboy Competition really hotted up, it was coming down to a three-horse race between All Kings, Westchester and the old enemy St David's. All three teams were on similar points and the only good thing for Bootsie and the All Kings boys was their team was finding their lost form again and the other two teams were losing theirs. Both Westchester and St David's had excellent starts to the season and it was due to this reason that they were still in the race to the finish. All Kings on the other hand had a terrible start to the season and were leaving their run home until late into the race.

On top of this, the All Kings boys had somehow managed to make it into the final 16 teams of the Super Challenge Cup, but all the extra rugby games had taken their toll on the boys. Bootsie's ankle was giving him a hard time again and it hadn't hurt like this for quite a while, even the extra strapping each week wasn't helping anymore. There were eight teams left after the pool rounds, which soon became four, then two, and one of those two final names was All Kings. The region's morning paper had a chart that showed the final eight teams in each group and their run home to the grand final. The boys had played in some tough games in this competition and they had only once played a team that Bootsie knew and that was the easy game against the Bulldogs. As All Kings moved along the chart each round on one side, there was another team that did the same on the other side, that team was the feared Central Cobras. The Cobras were a very well known club in the region and alongside the North Coast Sharks produced the most regional players. Bootsie had never played before on a team that could beat the Cobras.

The Monday before the game Bootsie made sure he grabbed a copy of the morning paper first, to which no one argued. He studied the sports section and found what he was looking for.
"Here it is," he said to himself, "Grand Final game, senior schoolboys age-group. All Kings V Central Cobras. Alright! They made it through," he said excitedly. "Finally, a chance to beat them," he added.

At training during the week Bootsie and his senior teammates were really struggling. Along with the extra games in the new Super Challenge Cup they had also played extra games on the overseas tour as well. Bootsie had played in every game and one extra one as well and he was really feeling the effects of it. The boys had the Super Challenge Cup final this week against the Cobras and on top of that, the big clash next week with a St David's team who could win the Skelton Shield and no bonus points would get in the way this year. It was going to be a do or die game against the fast finishing St David's who had somehow regathered some of their earlier form and it came down to All Kings or them and the winner of that game would win the shield for this year. Bootsie thought about the St David's game and only hoped his tiring body would even make it to that game. Thankfully the training sessions during the week were very light and it gave the boys some chance to recover from a long season of rugby.

On Saturday morning there were five buses crammed with boys from All Kings, all eager to make their way to the region's main rugby stadium. It was a huge venue and thankfully for Bootsie he had played there before with the regional team so he was super confident. There were going to be many games played on the day and it would finish that night with the first grade clash between the country-based Eastern Rams and the glamour club of the region the North Coast Sharks that Bootsie knew all too well. The All Kings game was just after lunch and kicked off at 1.40 in the afternoon. The crowd had built quite nicely at the stadium by the time the senior All Kings boys took to the field. One section of the crowd was very All Kings friendly and the sea of black, yellow and green streamers and ribbons was a welcome sight. Bootsie sucked in some deep breaths as he stood on the field and knew it wasn't going to be an easy game. Although the Super Challenge Cup was a new tournament, it did seem to bring the two best teams together in each division. The Cobras had narrowly beaten St David's in the semi finals and All Kings also had a brutal encounter with a team called the West Coast Pigs. It was a team that Bootsie had never heard of before and never wanted to hear of again, after the dirty tactics they had used. All that was behind them and now they had the Cobras team in front of them. Both teams desperately wanted to win the Super Challenge Cup and add it to their trophy cabinet.

From the opening minutes of the game it was a hard and very physical contest. The Cobras lived up to their reputation; they soon showed they were a fast and flashy team. What they *didn't* have was a pack like All Kings had assembled; the game was a battle between a fast backline on one team and a bruising forward pack on the other. As a combined team they would have been unstoppable, but on separate teams it made for a very entertaining game, the Cobras used every opportunity to get the ball out to the backs and use their much faster runners and All Kings did everything they could to keep the ball with the forwards and drive it up the middle one phase at a time. At half time the score was an amazing All Kings 0, Cobras 0. Bootsie was exhausted as he sat in the change rooms at half time and as he looked around he could see he wasn't the only one who was hurting. The coach tried to rev the boys up for one last time, but he knew it was up to them if they wanted any glory today. As the boys took to the field he knew he had taken them as far as he could, the rest was up to them.

For the next thirty minutes the two teams battled it out, like a test match trophy was up for grabs. Neither team could take the upper hand and it soon became a shootout for penalties as tired players were hanging onto balls in the tackle, or diving onto rucks or other things that tired and exhausted players do. The score was tied up at 12 all and there wasn't long to go at all. The constant use of their backs had worn them down and the Cobras were now running at half speed. Bootsie's tactic to keep the ball with the forwards had kept the legs of his backs very fresh and they soon began finding valuable holes in the defence and making good ground up field. The ball became unplayable inside the Cobras 22 and as the All Kings boys were attacking, they were awarded the scrum feed. Bootsie was extremely pumped after the referee's decision and begged his forwards for one more big effort.

"Just one more," he shouted.

"Just one more," he shouted again. The two packs smashed into each other and Bootsie felt his ankle roll, even with the pain shooting up his leg he pushed like his life was depending on it. What seemed like an even contest, soon turned into an All Kings scrum moving forward. Bootsie could see the 5-metre line going under his feet as well as the ball and he knew they were close when he heard the referee shout, "Advantage All Kings, offside at the scrum," as the scrum collapsed around him. He quickly got to his feet and ran towards another ruck out near the touchline, which was still on the 5-metre line. As he ran to the back of the ruck Harves was screaming at him to get ready and charge the line. Harves reached into the back of the ruck and handed Bootsie the ball.

As he did so, the referee shouted, "Offside. New penalty advantage to All Kings." Bootsie ignored the referee and bashed his tired and broken body into the line of defenders and managed to get the ball down on the line. Harves began screaming at the referee about where the ball was. It only took the referee a second of kneeling down and looking before he put the whistle to his mouth, threw his hand up in the air and shouted, "TRY!" By the time the conversion was taken, time had run out and the game was over. Bootsie had scored the winning try and captained All Kings to the first-ever win of the senior schoolboys Super Challenge Cup. Bootsie looked up, pointed at the sky with a winning finger, put his other hand over his heart and said, "That win was for you. Finally, we beat the Cobras, together." None of the other boys on the team would have known how special it was for Bootsie to finally beat the Cobras, but there were two people up there looking down on him with huge smiles on their faces as well.

The boys were considered heroes back at the school and the press had never been so good to Bootsie. Unfortunately Bootsie had really hurt his ankle again and after playing so bravely in so many games he couldn't take to the field the following week. Despite a brave battle, St David's were just too good against a very injury-ravaged All Kings team and that loss was the only downside on what had been a great year. Bootsie still couldn't believe he had captained the team to win the Super Challenge Cup, but in doing so, had really lifted the name of the school back up to where it should be.

Before Bootsie knew it, his school days at All Kings were over. He had had some wonderful times as well as some awful ones, but looking back, he had a lot more good ones than bad. Even *he* was surprised with how well he had done in his final exams, it would put him in good stead for any university course he planned on doing. He had also made some great friends especially in Razzi who he hated saying goodbye to.

"It's not goodbye, just see you another time," is what Razzi said to him when they had to say goodbye to each other on the last day. "Geez you're not going to cry are you big fella?" Razzi jokingly asked Bootsie. "Of course not!" replied Bootsie fighting to hold back the tears. Even he wasn't prepared for this. "Wow, this is a lot harder than I had anticipated," added Bootsie.

"Just don't be a stranger," Razzi said with a warm smile as he grabbed his friend for a final goodbye embrace. "Yep," was all Bootsie could say in return in a very choked-up voice.

The headmaster gave Bootsie a glowing reference to take away with him for any future Universities he might apply for, which he would. The most special person at the school for Bootsie was his coach. He had played under some good coaches but none were anywhere near as good as this one.

"Bootsie, I see a lot of me in you when I was your age. You've got a huge heart," he said to Bootsie as he handed him an envelope.

"What's this?" Bootsie asked, as he took it from his hand.

"It's a national schoolboys selection letter, you've been selected for the upcoming tour, although when I first got it I wasn't even sure *who* it was for. I always assumed Bootsie was your real name."

"I can't believe it," replied Bootsie, as he stood there reading the letter for himself with a smile on his face from ear to ear. "I don't know how to thank you," he said to his coach.

"Just play well for the national team in a few weeks. I got a phone call this morning and they want me to coach you guys and I said yes," replied the coach with a smile as big as Bootsie's. The two of them said goodbye to each other and knew they would see each other again soon enough. As they went their separate ways the coach turned to Bootsie and said, "Hey, by the way what *is* your real name again?" Bootsie turned to the coach and said, "It's Connor. My real name is Connor."

The End.

Check out the Bootsie website
www.bootsiebooks.com

Thanks to KooGa Rugby
www.kooga.com.au

Lightning Source UK Ltd.
Milton Keynes UK
UKOW04f1955060116

265946UK00001B/22/P